Pet Corner

LOVABLE DOGS

By Katie Kawa

Gareth Stevens
Publishing

Please visit our website, www.garethstevens.com. For a free color catalog of all our high-quality books, call toll free 1-800-542-2595 or fax 1-877-542-2596.

Library of Congress Cataloging-in-Publication Data

Kawa, Katie.
Lovable dogs / Katie Kawa.
    p. cm. — (Pet corner)
ISBN 978-1-4339-5593-8 (pbk.)
ISBN 978-1-4339-5594-5 (6-pack)
ISBN 978-1-4339-5591-4 (library binding)
1. Dogs—Juvenile literature. I. Title.
SF426.5.K39 2011
636.7—dc22

                                        2010050029

First Edition

Published in 2012 by
Gareth Stevens Publishing
111 East 14th Street, Suite 349
New York, NY 10003

Editor: Katie Kawa
Designer: Andrea Davison-Bartolotta

Photo credits: Cover, pp. 5, 7, 9, 11, 13, 17, 19, 21, 23, 24 (coat, paws) Shutterstock.com; p. 1 iStockphoto.com; pp. 15, 24 (bone) Chris Amaral/Photodisc/Thinkstock.

Printed in the United States of America

CPSIA compliance information: Batch #CS11GS: For further information contact Gareth Stevens, New York, New York at 1-800-542-2595.

Contents

A dog wags its tail.
It is happy.

Dogs learn many
fun tricks. They like
to roll over.

A dog has lots of fur.
This is called a coat.

A person brushes a dog's coat. This keeps it soft.

A dog has a wet nose.
This helps it smell
very well.

13

A dog chews a bone.
It cleans its teeth.

A dog has four feet.
They are called paws.

A dog needs to play
every day.

19

A dog plays fetch.
A person throws a ball
and the dog brings
it back.

Words to Know

bone

coat

paws

Index

Dogs love to play outside!